First American Edition 2003
by Kane/Miller Book Publishers
La Jolla, California

Originally published in Denmark as *En støvle faldt fra himlen*
(with illustrations by Tord Nygren).
© Peter Hammer Verlag GmbH
Wuppertal, Germany 2001

Library of Congress Control Number: 2002112562

Printed and bound in Singapore by Tien Wah Press (Pte.), Ltd.

1 2 3 4 5 6 7 8 9 10

ISBN 1-929321-45-X

Kåre Bluitgen

A Boot Fell From Heaven

with illustrations by **Chiara Carrer**

Kane/Miller
BOOK PUBLISHERS

It has finally stopped raining.
There are puddles on the lower clouds.
God is sitting on the edge of one,
admiring a rainbow, when suddenly...

11

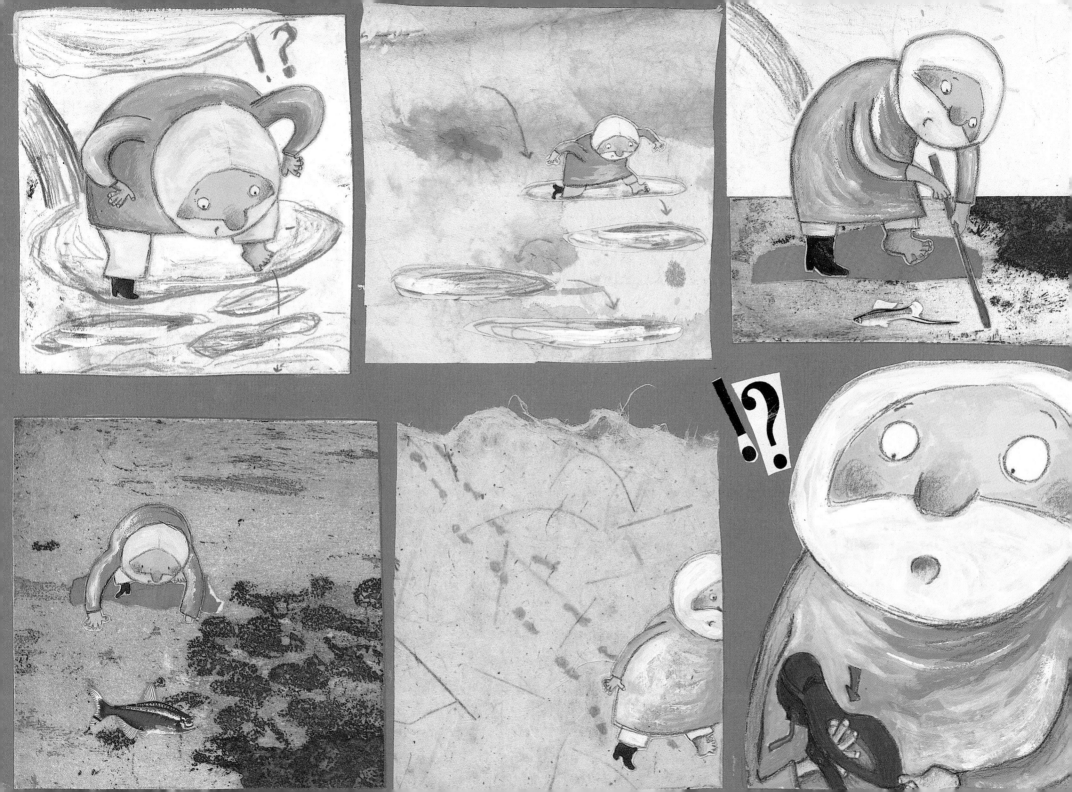

...one of His boots falls off. "Oh no!" He gasps. The cloud is slippery, and He doesn't see where the boot lands. Now God must go down and find it. He's had the boots for ages and has grown very fond of them.

"How do you do, Sir? I am God. Could you tell me please, have you found a boot? I think it must be around here somewhere."

"Watch it! Do you think the rules don't apply to you? Keep off the grass! If you lost a boot here, it would have been taken to the dump."

He tells another man who He is and what has happened. "To cut a long story short," God says, "I was a little inattentive." But the man is in a hurry and keeps looking at his watch. "Yes, yes, it's a good story...here, buy yourself a cup of coffee."

"Good Lord," a lady sniffs, and passes by in a hurry.

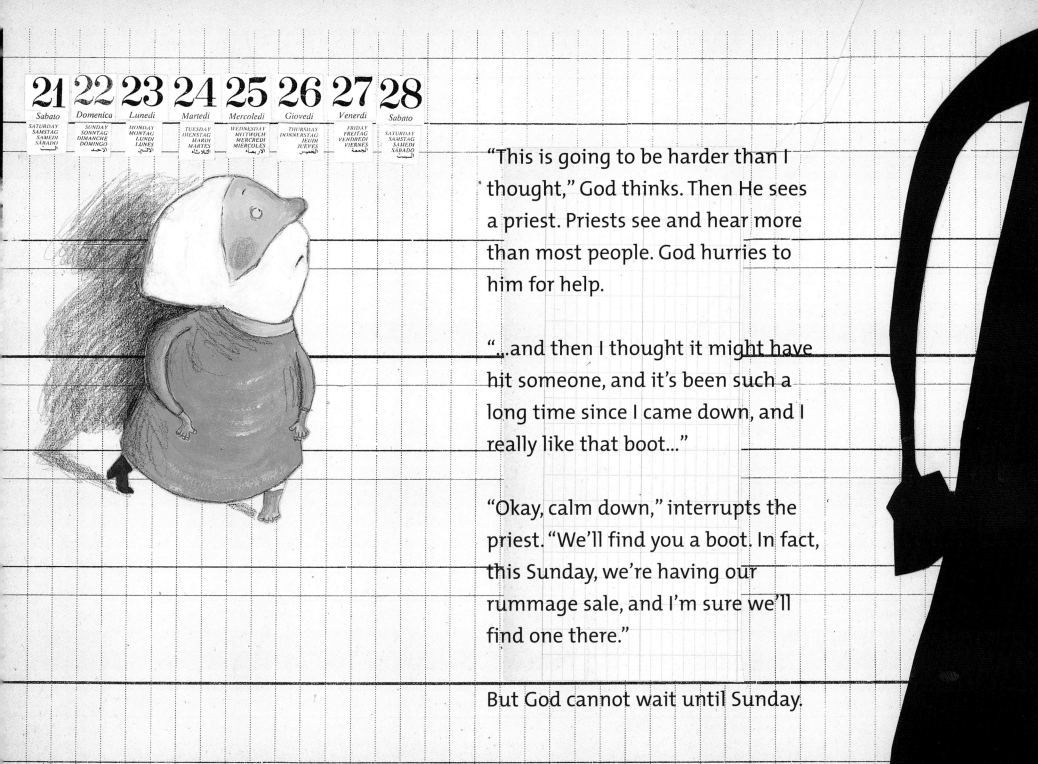

21 Sabato SATURDAY SAMSTAG SAMEDI SÁBADO

22 Domenica SUNDAY SONNTAG DIMANCHE DOMINGO

23 Lunedi MONDAY MONTAG LUNDI LUNES

24 Martedi TUESDAY DIENSTAG MARDI MARTES

25 Mercoledi WEDNESDAY MITTWOCH MERCREDI MIÉRCOLES

26 Giovedi THURSDAY DONNERSTAG JEUDI JUEVES

27 Venerdi FRIDAY FREITAG VENDREDI VIERNES

28 Sabato SATURDAY SAMSTAG SAMEDI SÁBADO

"This is going to be harder than I thought," God thinks. Then He sees a priest. Priests see and hear more than most people. God hurries to him for help.

"...and then I thought it might have hit someone, and it's been such a long time since I came down, and I really like that boot..."

"Okay, calm down," interrupts the priest. "We'll find you a boot. In fact, this Sunday, we're having our rummage sale, and I'm sure we'll find one there."

But God cannot wait until Sunday.

Back in town, He happens to pass a shop with shelves piled high with forgotten glasses, lost umbrellas, and missing parrots.

"Maybe some kind person found my boot and turned it in here," God thinks, as He goes inside. The man behind the desk is not particularly friendly.

"Anyone could come in here and claim to have lost something," the man says. "Before I look, can you prove that this boot is yours? Do you have a receipt?"

Of course God doesn't have a receipt. He must keep looking.

He sees another store, filled with every kind of shoe and boot. "Excuse me, do you have a boot like this?..."

"Well, yes. We have almost everything. Italian leather boots, Turkish peaked shoes, Chinese laced shoes, oh, and this absolutely divine pair of sandals. Genuine alligator. Would you like to pay by check?"

"No, no, I'm not from here. I'm God, and I..."

"God? Well, if you're not local, you'll have to pay cash."

But God only has the few coins the man in a hurry gave Him. "A few coins don't seem to go very far here on Earth," He thinks. And He hobbles on.

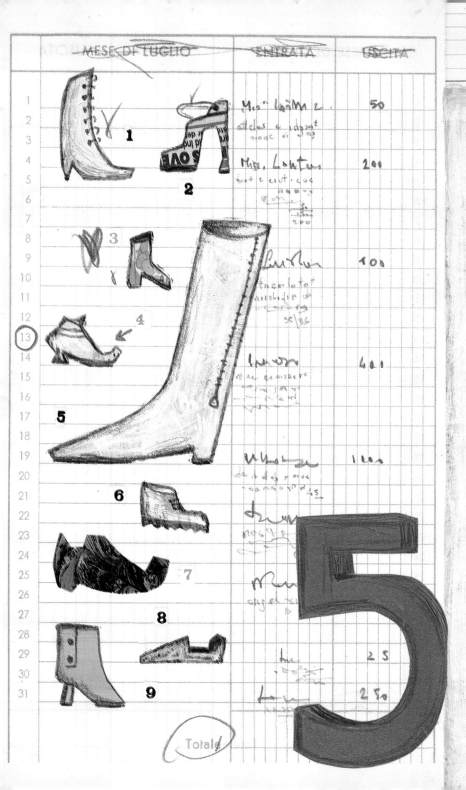

God's feet are getting tired. His head feels tired, too. Plus, He's getting a blister. Finally, He sees a place where they may be able to help Him.

"Oh, your poor feet," the woman says. "Have you been wearing shoes that don't fit? You must appreciate your feet the way our Lord created them."

"That's exactly it..." God begins.

"Yes, exactly," she says. "We can make the perfect boots for you, with extra support and comfort insoles, for less than you might expect. It should only take a couple of days."

"But I only need one boot," God says, "and I need it now."

As God leaves the store, He runs into a big crowd. People are shouting and calling. "A parade!" God thinks.

"I don't think you want to be here," a man suddenly says, and grabs God.

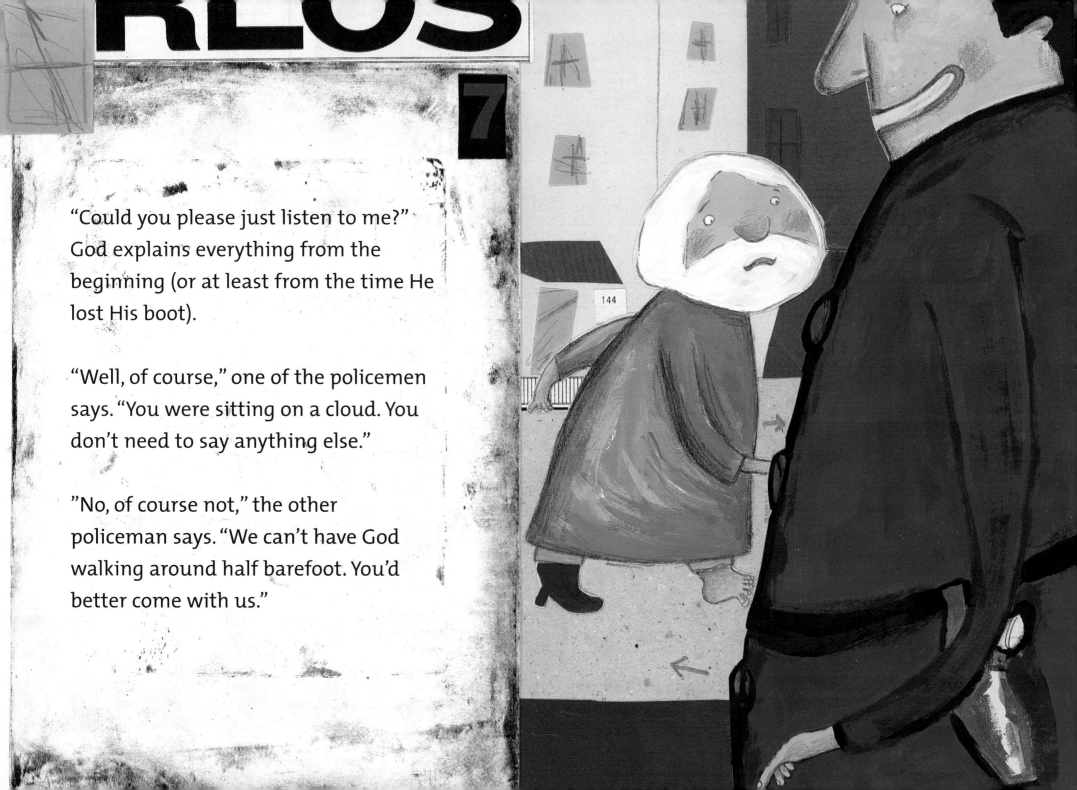

"Could you please just listen to me?" God explains everything from the beginning (or at least from the time He lost His boot).

"Well, of course," one of the policemen says. "You were sitting on a cloud. You don't need to say anything else."

"No, of course not," the other policeman says. "We can't have God walking around half barefoot. You'd better come with us."

"Now, you can sleep here tonight," the first policeman says. "Just ring that bell if you remember your real name and address," says the other. "Tomorrow we'll take you to a nice place where you can meet Napoleon and Caesar and a lot of other people who think they're God too."

"But I'm just looking for my boot," God tries to tell them.

"There is also a very nice doctor there, and you can have a talk with him." The policemen smile as they walk down the hall. God can hear them laughing, and they are fooling around so much that they don't realize they've forgotten to lock the door.

2018

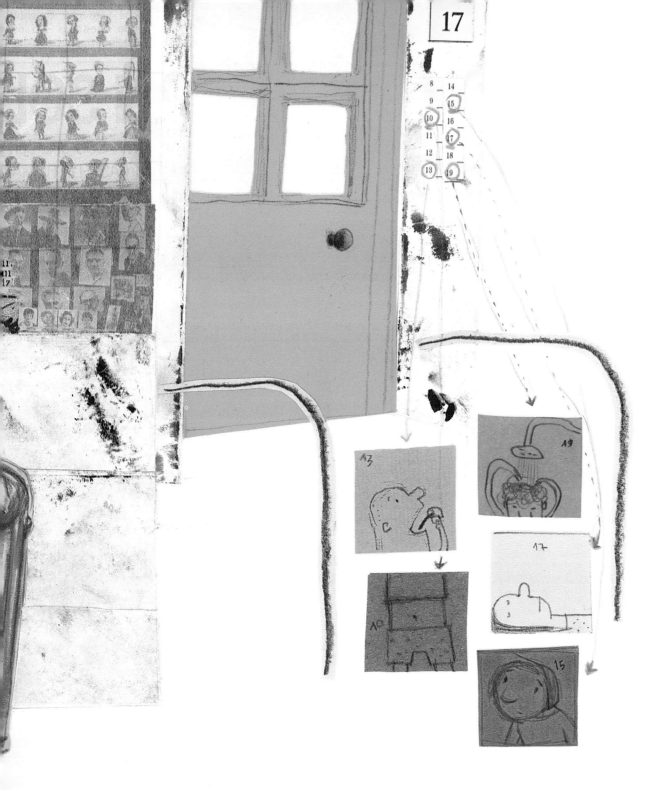

When it gets dark, God takes off His one boot and tiptoes softly away. Outside, He puts the boot back on. One foot is warm and dry, the other, wet and cold.

"I never imagined the world to be like this," He thinks. He walks through the night, leaving funny footprints as the day begins.

"What a busy world. Nobody has time to listen. Nobody knows who I am, or cares."

"Aren't you God?" asks a boy, yawning.

"Me? God?"

"Yes. I was here yesterday, and I saw a boot falling from the sky. Nobody but God could lose a boot like that. I kept it for you."

And the boy gives God His boot. He knew God would come for it. And he wants to hear about God's adventures trying to find it. He has lots of time to listen.

All the time in the world.